Kimi and the
Land of Feathers

Also by Eszter Molnar and Anita Bagdi

The Cow Who Didn't Like The View

The Clown's Clothes

Kimi and the
Land of Feathers

Eszter Molnar

Illustrated by Anita Bagdi

This edition published 2021 by Maisie's Reading Corner

www.maisiesreadingcorner.co.uk

ISBN: 978-1-9998906-1-2

Printed in the UK

For Lujza, Lenke, Maisie and Domi

Chapter 1

KIMI HARRIS WAS trying to zip up her suit-case. She let out a frustrated sigh and tugged at the stuck zip.

"Hurry up, we need to go!" her mum called from the front porch.

Kimi's dad appeared in the doorway. "Do you need a hand?"

"Yes, please," Kimi said gratefully.

Her dad zipped up her suitcase and carried it downstairs. Kimi grabbed her sunglasses and followed him, a spring in her step.

Kimi's mum and her little brother, Felix, were already in the car.

"Finally!" her mum laughed.

"I know, I know, but I'm here now," said Kimi, climbing in next to Felix and ruffling his hair. "Let's go!"

Like they did every year, Kimi and her family were spending the summer holidays in a holiday park in the forest of Bambaloor. They had a log cabin among the majestic trees. Kimi could hardly wait to get there.

Bambaloor was a charming, peaceful place but strange things had been happening there lately. Kimi had overheard her mum and dad talking about mysterious footprints all over Bambaloor, especially around the old, abandoned mill. And that's not all … apparently, most mornings, a woman could be heard singing, her mesmerising voice waking up the whole forest. And on top of that, lots of items had gone missing from the holiday park!

It was a long drive to the forest but the time flew by – Kimi's dad kept them entertained with his terrible singing and even more terrible jokes. They stopped a couple of times to stretch their legs and to have something to eat and drink.

Finally, the entrance to Bambaloor came into view.

"We're here!" shouted Felix.

Kimi and Felix got out of the car and raced down the path that led to their log cabin. Many other families had also arrived that afternoon. Everyone was busy unloading their cars, and excited chatter filled the air. Kimi waved to a few familiar faces then waited impatiently for her mum to unlock the front door.

The log cabin wasn't big, but it was perfect nonetheless. It was warm and bright and every nook and cranny was filled with cushions, books and toys. It really was the most comfortable place.

At home, Kimi was glad she didn't have to share a room with her brother. But here, deep in the forest, she didn't mind at all. Kimi and Felix always flipped a coin to decide who got to sleep on the top bunk. This year, Felix had won.

"Better luck next time." He grinned as he scrambled up to the top bunk. Kimi playfully threw a cushion at him then kicked off her shoes and flung herself on the bottom bunk.

"This is the most special place in the whole wide world," she said. "I couldn't imagine spending our holidays anywhere else."

The following morning, Kimi's dad and Felix went swimming. Kimi's mum had fallen asleep on the sofa while reading a magazine. Kimi was writing in her diary when she heard a knock at the door. Outside, she expected to see one of her friends from last summer but, much to her surprise, when she opened the door there was nobody there!

Maybe it was just the wind. Kimi shrugged as she closed the door and returned to her desk.

But a few moments later she heard the same sound. "It's definitely not the wind. It *is* the door!"

she muttered as she hurried across the room. But once again, there was nobody there.

Kimi was about to close the door when she noticed something on the doormat. She bent down and picked it up. It was a neatly folded piece of paper.

It said *To Kimi* on it in the most beautiful handwriting she had ever seen. And right under her name, someone had drawn a delicate little feather.

Confused, Kimi wrinkled her nose and unfolded the crisp white paper.

Dear Kimi,

I need your help!

Meet me at the pond in the clearing by the edge of the forest tomorrow at noon.

Please keep this a secret!

Your grateful friend,

L

Chapter 2

KIMI'S HEAD WAS spinning. *Who was L? How did L know her name? Was L in some kind of trouble?* As she couldn't see anyone near the log cabin, she went back inside and read the letter over and over again.

A little while later, Kimi heard Felix and her dad
returning. She jumped up and hid the letter under
her pillow, then grabbed a book and pretended to
be reading it.

"The pool wasn't cold at all," cried Felix as soon
as he saw Kimi. "You should've come with us – it
was great!"

"It's a lot warmer than last year," her dad called
from the bathroom, where he was hanging up their
wet towels.

"Maybe I'll come next time," Kimi replied half-heartedly, still thinking about the mysterious note.

"So what have you been up to?" he asked.

Kimi didn't like keeping secrets from her family, but L had asked her not to mention anything to anyone ...

"Oh, nothing much. Just reading and writing in my diary."

"That sounds like fun too," her dad said.

Kimi's mum, feeling refreshed after her nap, popped her head around the door. "Are you ready for our picnic?"

"Sure," said Kimi.

Felix was already out the door. "Come on, you lot, I'm starving!"

"Stop singing, Felix!" Kimi groaned and pulled the duvet over her head. "It's too early. I want to sleep!"

"It's not me!" Felix peered over the edge of the top bunk and stared at Kimi. "It's coming from outside."

Kimi sat bolt upright. *Oh, wow. The strange singing – this is one of the three mysteries of Bambaloor!* she thought excitedly.

Kimi and Felix leapt out of bed and pressed their noses against the steamed-up window, but all they could see was a group of holidaymakers in their pyjamas. Everyone was wondering the same thing – where was the singing coming from?

Kimi couldn't quite make out the words of the song, but it had a glorious melody. The clear voice sounded so beautiful, it was almost angelic.

"Who could it be?" asked Felix, rubbing his eyes.

Kimi yawned. "I have no idea."

Felix pulled up a chair and sat down by the window, hoping to catch a glimpse of the mysterious singer. Kimi draped a blanket over her brother's shoulders then crawled back into her warm bed. But she was too excited to go back to sleep. She was counting down the hours until she met L.

Chapter 3

S HORTLY BEFORE NOON, Kimi finally set off
towards the edge of the forest. As she reached
the pond in the clearing, instead of L, she
found another note pinned to a tree.

Kimi took the note and carried on. Everyone in Bambaloor knew the crooked tree. It was one of the oldest trees in the forest, with tyre swings hanging from its gigantic branches.

Fortunately, there were no children playing there that day. She didn't want anyone to know where she was going. She followed the left-hand path until she found another note, this time on a mossy tree stump.

Come to the hunter's lodge. L

Kimi grabbed the note and quickened her pace. She was nearly there.

When Kimi got to the hunter's lodge, she looked around but she couldn't see anyone. The forest was eerily quiet. Dried leaves crunched under her shoes as she cautiously approached the lodge.

She put her ear against the door but couldn't hear anything. "Hello? Is anybody here?" she whispered.

"Come in," replied a friendly voice.

Kimi took a deep, calming breath then pushed the door open. She found herself face-to-face with a pretty girl in a long blue dress. Her eyes were clear and her smile was bright. White feathers sparkled in her long hair.

"Hi Kimi, I'm Leena," she said as she gently took Kimi's hand. "Thank you for coming. Did anybody see you on your way to the lodge?"

"I don't think so, no."

"Good." Leena smiled at her.

"How do you know my name?" Kimi asked.

"I promise I'll tell you everything," Leena said in a quiet voice. She gestured towards a blanket in the corner of the gloomy lodge. They sat down. Kimi crossed her legs and looked at Leena expectantly.

"I'm a Featherling and I come from the Land of Feathers," Leena began.

"The Land of Feathers?" whispered Kimi. "I've never heard of it."

"We live far away from here … in a secret place," Leena continued.

Kimi's eyes widened. "A secret place?"

"Yes," said Leena. "You see, we're hiding from someone. From someone very dangerous."

Kimi could see that Leena was finding it difficult to continue; she had tears in her eyes. "Who is it? Who are you hiding from?" she prompted Leena gently.

"From the Featherlings' cruellest enemy." Leena

sighed. "Her name's Lark." She stood up and began to pace around the lodge. "If Lark discovers where we live, she'll attack us. She'll banish our beloved Featherqueen so she can become our new ruler. We can't let that happen!"

Kimi gasped. "That's horrible."

"It is," Leena agreed as she sat down opposite Kimi again. "And that's why I'm here. You, Kimi, are the only person who can save the Featherlings from Lark."

"Me? But I don't know how to help you," said Kimi. "You must be mistaken."

Leena held up her hands and shook her head. "The Featherqueen often has dreams that predict the future. And in one of her dreams, she saw *you* as the saviour of the Featherlings."

Kimi was speechless. She needed a few moments to gather her thoughts. "What can I do?" she eventually said. "How can I help the Featherlings?"

"We need you to find a new hiding place for a very special book."

Kimi's mouth fell open. This was not what she had expected to hear.

"This book is called *The Feathers of Wisdom*," Leena explained slowly. "It's our big book of knowledge, full of important secrets and ancient spells."

"And where's this book now?" asked Kimi. "Is it with you, in your secret hiding place?"

"No," said Leena. "It's hidden far away from our home. We can't risk Lark finding us *and* the book at the same time. If she gets her hands on it, she'll be even more powerful than she is now."

"I see," said Kimi. "That makes sense."

"Lark's been searching for us for a long time now but she can't find us. So now she's turned her attention to finding *The Feathers of Wisdom* instead. And once she finds that book, she'll know where we are. Our lives would change for the worse."

"The *book* knows where you live?" cried Kimi. "That's amazing!"

"It knows everything," said Leena. "That's why Lark wants it. And she's very close to finding it. We need to move the book to a new hiding place as quickly as possible."

Kimi's heart began to beat faster. She felt so excited and proud to have been chosen to help Leena and the Featherlings. "But there's one thing I don't understand," she said, leaning closer to Leena. "Can't the Featherlings think of a safe hiding place for the book?"

"We've tried. Over and over," Leena reassured her. "But the Elders, the wisest Featherlings in our land, decided that none of the places were good enough. None of them were safe enough. You're our only hope ..."

"I'll do my best," Kimi promised her new friend, who threw her arms around her.

"Thank you, Kimi! You don't know how happy that makes me. Oh, I almost forgot to mention something else." Leena chuckled. "Something rather important!"

"What's that?"

"Featherlings are invisible to everyone in your

world. To everyone but you."

"Invisible?" Kimi gasped.

"That's right," said Leena. "That's why I asked you to meet me here, far away from everyone else. I didn't realise how busy it can get around the pond in the summer."

A wide grin spread across Kimi's face. *If no one else can see Leena, people will think I'm talking to myself!* "When I was little," she said, "I pretended to have an invisible friend. Her name was Samantha. And now I really do have an invisible friend." She couldn't stop smiling. "This is fantastic!"

Chapter 4

KIMI COULDN'T STOP thinking about Leena and *The Feathers of Wisdom* when she got back to her log cabin. She even asked Felix where he would hide his favourite toy. His answer – *Under my bed!* – wasn't as helpful as Kimi had hoped.

After breakfast the following morning, Kimi told her mum she was going to spend the day with a new friend.

"Why don't you invite her over for dinner tonight?" her mum said. "We'd love to meet her."

"Thanks but Leena's invi—" she began, then quickly corrected herself. "I mean, she's a little bit shy. Maybe next time?"

"Sure," her mum replied. "Have fun!"

Phew! That was close! Kimi thought as she hurried towards the hunter's lodge. But she didn't get far. Leena was waiting for her by the crooked tree. She was wringing her hands and her voice trembled as she greeted Kimi.

Kimi looked around anxiously. "Leena, what are you doing out here?"

"Something terrible has happened! Lark was seen not far from the tower where we're hiding *The Feathers of Wisdom*. The guard in the tower said she looked more furious than ever. She's closer than we thought, Kimi!"

"I've thought of a list of possible hiding places," said Kimi, hoping to cheer Leena up. "Here."

Leena skimmed through Kimi's list and her face lit up. "Perfect! The Elders can't wait to see this. We need to go *now*!"

"Go where?"

"To the tower! We've got to move the book as soon as possible," Leena explained. "Follow me."

21

Leena led Kimi back towards the log cabins. Kimi spotted Felix and her dad leaving to play football. She ducked behind a tree and waited for them to pass. Thankfully, they didn't see her.

"Where are we going? How are we going to get to the Land of Feathers?" Kimi wondered aloud as they continued on their way. "We're not going to walk there, are we?"

Leena stopped walking. "We're going to the only place in your world from where we can enter the Land of Feathers. Think of it as a magic door between your world and mine ..."

"But there's nothing here!" Kimi exclaimed as

she looked around the forest. "There's only trees and bushes and—" Kimi stopped mid-sentence as she noticed something in the distance.

Leena followed her friend's gaze and nodded slowly. "That's it, Kimi. You've found it."

"The abandoned mill," Kimi whispered. "Leena, are you sure about this? Haven't you heard the rumours about this mill?"

"What rumours?" asked Leena.

Kimi wiped her clammy hands on her dress and lowered her voice. "Footprints have been found there … lots of them … but no one ever goes inside the mill! It's all very spooky. No one knows who they belong to."

Leena threw her head back and laughed. "You mean, *my* footprints?" She lifted her long dress a little. She was barefoot. "Featherlings don't wear shoes!" she said as she wriggled her toes.

Kimi's mouth fell open and she shook her head in disbelief. Leena slipped her arm under Kimi's and gave her a gentle nudge.

"There are no monsters out here, only me. I've been waiting for you in that mill for weeks. I knew you would come; I just didn't know *when.*"

Kimi had so many questions swirling around in her head, but she knew that Leena was eager to get to the mill as quickly as possible. "Let's go then!" she said.

They pushed open the mill door.

Kimi shuddered as she smelled the dampness of the room. As some of the windows were boarded up, her eyes needed time to adjust to the darkness. After a while, Kimi looked around, disappointed. All she could see were grimy old sacks, barrels and broken furniture.

This doesn't look like a magic door at all ... it's just a mill. Kimi turned to Leena, who had closed and bolted the heavy oak door behind them. "How are we going to get to the tower?"

Leena reached inside her pocket. "With these!" She pulled out a handful of glittering yellow feathers.

Kimi took a step closer and gazed admiringly at the beautiful feathers. "What are these?"

"Skyfeathers!"

With a gentle flick of her wrist, Leena threw the Skyfeathers up in the air. At first the feathers whirled round and round above their heads. And then, one feather after another, they slowly engulfed them.

The room began to spin and everything became

a blur. Kimi wrapped her arms around herself.

"Close your eyes," said Leena. "We'll be there in no time ..."

Chapter 5

"W E'RE HERE," SAID Leena. "You can open your eyes now."

Kimi slowly opened her eyes. The Skyfeathers were gone and so was the old mill. They were standing in a chilly room that was empty apart from a few chairs, which were arranged neatly in a circle.

She could hardly contain her excitement. "Are we in the tower? In the Land of Feathers?"

Leena nodded. "We are. And this here," she pointed at a tall man with kind eyes, "is the Featherprince."

The Featherprince approached Kimi and bowed deeply. Like Leena, he was barefoot and the front of his thick, green robe was decorated with golden feathers. "Welcome to the Land of Feathers."

Kimi's eyes sparkled with glee. She could hardly believe it – a real prince!

Leena gave the Featherprince Kimi's list of hiding places for *The Feathers of Wisdom*.

The Elders, who had been standing quietly at the back of the room, rushed forward to gather around the Featherprince. Kimi thought they looked rather peculiar. Their beards sparkled with feathers and their robes were so long, they trailed along the floor behind them. The Elders and the Featherprince immediately began to discuss Kimi's ideas.

"This could take a while," said Leena. "Come, I'll show you something."

Kimi followed her to a large, dirty window and was instantly mesmerised by the sight before her: hundreds, if not thousands, of towers as far as the eye could see!

"These were once the homes of Featherlings," Leena explained. "But over time, the towers were gradually abandoned as the Featherlings moved further south."

"Why? What's in the south?" said Kimi. "Is that where you live too?"

Leena sighed deeply. "Not anymore. The south was once the most prosperous part of the Land of Feathers. It was unspoilt and peaceful – until Lark ruined it all. And then, because of what she did, Lark was banished from court by her father, the seventh king of our land."

"Lark is a Featherling?" Kimi cried, taken aback.

"She is." Leena bit her lip as she struggled to hold back the tears. "And now she knows that *The Feathers of Wisdom* is hidden in one of these towers. She's searching every tower from top to bottom."

"Why was Lark banished?" asked Kimi. "What did she do?"

"She was making our lives a misery. She was forever scheming and plotting to gain more power among the Featherlings. It's not in her nature to be kind. The day she was banished, Lark poisoned our wells and lakes and burnt our homes to the ground. We had no choice but to leave the south."

Kimi shuddered at the thought of someone so cruel.

"Lark vowed to find us wherever we go. She blames everyone but herself for her misfortune," Leena continued. "She wants revenge and she wants to rule us all."

"And the Featherlings have been hiding from Lark all this time?" said Kimi.

"That's right. But *The Feathers of Wisdom* can lead her straight to us, and I dread to think what will happen once she finds us ..."

Kimi looked out the window again. She couldn't imagine living in hiding.

Leena pointed to a nearby tower. "And this morning, Lark was seen right there. She's getting closer."

"And where's she now?" said Kimi.

"Gathering her strength. She'll be back very soon."

A loud cheer erupted. Kimi and Leena spun on their heels.

"The Elders have agreed on the book's new hiding place," said Leena.

The Featherprince smiled at Kimi. "You're a very clever girl."

Kimi beamed with pride.

"We've decided to hide the book in Lark's castle – right under her nose!" said the Featherprince.

"Not even the wisest Featherlings could come up with such a brilliant idea!" exclaimed one of the Elders.

"It's exactly like the Featherqueen's dream had predicted … you have saved us," said Leena. "Thank you, Kimi."

"Don't mention it. That's what friends are for!"

"Can I ask you a question?" Kimi said to the Featherprince.

"Anything."

"Where's the book now?"

"It's hidden inside the walls of this tower," he replied. "It's behind a fireplace, to be precise."

Kimi followed the Featherlings to a narrow room with an arched fireplace. Their footsteps echoed loudly in the vast room. The Featherprince and the Elders dropped to their knees and began to dismantle the fireplace.

"It's there, look!" said the Featherprince.

Kimi peered into the wall cavity.

"Go on, Kimi," he said kindly. "Take it out."

"May I?"

"Of course."

Kimi carefully took the dusty book. "It's beautiful," she said, admiring the smooth, golden-brown cover. It was blank apart from a tiny leaf in the bottom-right corner.

The room was buzzing with excitement. Everyone looked relieved that *The Feathers of Wisdom* would soon be on its way to a safer hiding place.

But then something strange happened. The temperature in the room suddenly dropped and a chilly draught blew through the open door.

The Featherlings gasped in unison.

"What's happening?" Kimi asked nervously.

But before anyone could answer, she heard it too: heavy footsteps rushing up the stairs, followed by a woman's shrill voice.

"I know you're in here!" the woman cried.

A few moments later she entered the room and stood triumphantly in front of Kimi and the shaken Featherlings.

Kimi knew without a shadow of a doubt that this woman, in a dirty black dress, was none other than Lark!

Lark's eyes bore into Kimi's. "GIVE ME THE

BOOK!" she shrieked.

Kimi clutched the book even more tightly to her chest. Lark's eyes gleamed feverishly as she lunged forward.

"I said, give me the book!"

And then everything happened very fast. Leena grabbed Kimi and pulled her into her embrace. She reached into her pocket for Skyfeathers while the Elders and the Featherprince clumsily attempted to form a protective ring around them.

Leena hastily threw the Skyfeathers up in the air; they swiftly engulfed Leena and Kimi. And just as Lark was about to snatch the book out of Kimi's hand, they disappeared from the tower.

Chapter 6

KIMI AND LEENA landed outside a magnificent castle.

"What will happen to the Featherprince and the Elders?" Kimi asked anxiously. "Are they going to be all right?"

"Don't worry about them right now," said Leena. "They'll be fine. Their Skyfeathers will take them home."

Leena's reassuring words put Kimi at ease. She breathed a sigh of relief and turned her attention to the castle.

"*This* is Lark's home? It's stunning!"

The turrets and towers were delicate and

imposing at the same time. The huge stained-glass windows gleamed in the sun and the gardens looked wonderfully inviting.

"I've always wondered what her home looked like," said Leena, "but I never thought it would be this beautiful!"

Kimi rubbed the back of her neck and looked around.

Sensing Kimi's discomfort, Leena quickly put her hand on hers. "Lark doesn't have Skyfeathers – she can't get here this quickly. And besides, she doesn't know we're here, does she?"

"Have any of the Featherlings ever been here?" Kimi asked, her eyes glued to the castle gardens.

"No. We hardly ever leave the waterfall—"

"You live in a waterfall?" Kimi cried.

"Not exactly. We live – well, *behind* it. After Lark destroyed our homes in the south, the Featherqueen led us to one of the wettest regions of our land. We marched for days and days until we reached a wild waterfall that was cascading down rocks into a green pool."

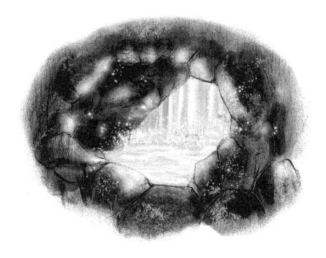

Kimi listened intently, mesmerised by Leena's

story.

"The Featherprince and the Elders set out to explore the rocks and the surrounding area. They soon found another waterfall, hidden behind the first waterfall. And there they discovered the entrance to the cave which became our new home."

"So that's the secret hiding place Lark's so desperate to find," Kimi whispered.

"Yes," said Leena as she touched the book in Kimi's hand. "But she can't find it without the help of *The Feathers of Wisdom*. This book is Lark's last hope of finding the Featherqueen. And she'll never stop searching for it."

The friends began to look for a way inside the castle grounds. As they did so, Leena wiped a tear from her eye.

"All this worrying about Lark has left the Featherqueen weak and frail," she said quietly. "If Lark finds us, she'll easily defeat the Featherqueen. She believes that *she* is the rightful heir to the throne."

"Why?"

"Because Lark is the Featherqueen's older sister," Leena explained. "But instead of Lark, in his will, the wise old king left everything to the Featherqueen."

"I can't say I'm surprised," said Kimi.

"Defeating and banishing her sister is the only way Lark can become the Featherqueen. And once she's our queen, we'll have no choice but to follow her. She would lead us to war, to suffering, to dark days … She would destroy the Featherlings."

Kimi and Leena soon found an unlocked gate

and slipped inside the garden. It was full of fragrant flowers, tinkling fountains and laden apple trees.

"This is the most beautiful place I've ever seen!" said Leena dreamily. "I wish *we* could live here."

"Leena, look, there's the back door. It's open!" Kimi had never been inside a castle before. Although she was still feeling a bit scared, she couldn't wait to enter the splendid building.

They stepped inside and found themselves in what looked like a cellar. Rickety shelves lined the walls. Most were empty. Everything was coated with cobwebs and the dust, thick and gritty, made them cough. They hurried to the staircase at the far end of the cellar and climbed the stairs until they reached a half-open door leading to a huge kitchen.

"It looks like Lark hasn't been home for a while," said Kimi, dusting off her hands.

"Where exactly should we hide the book?" asked Leena.

"How about Lark's bedroom? Under her bed?"

Leena clapped her hands together. "That's a

brilliant idea!"

"It's actually my little brother's idea," Kimi admitted. "I didn't like it at first, but the more I thought about it, the more sense it made."

"It'll *never* cross Lark's mind to look under her bed," Leena giggled with glee.

"So where do you think Lark's bedroom is?" said Kimi. "There must be hundreds of rooms in this place."

"That's easy," Leena said confidently. "Feather-lings always sleep in the highest room."

Each room they entered was more beautiful than the last. And there were paintings of Feather-lings everywhere.

"This is Lark's family," said Leena. "That's the Featherqueen over there."

"And there's the Featherprince," said Kimi, rec-ognising the young prince from the tower.

"He's the Featherqueen's son, our future king."

Kimi pointed to a painting of an old man with vibrant red feathers in his beard and on the front of his hooded gown. "Who's this? He looks—"

"Familiar?" guessed Leena.

Kimi nodded. "I have a feeling I've seen him before, though I know that's impossible."

"That was our dear old king. He's Lark's father. And the Featherqueen's, of course."

Kimi stood in front of the huge painting; it was twice her size. "Lark looks exactly like her father, doesn't she?"

"It's just a shame she's nowhere near as kind as him," said Leena.

There was one thing Kimi didn't quite understand. "After everything that's happened, why does Lark keep all these paintings of her family?"

"To remind herself where she belongs," replied Leena. "She won't rest until she rules us all. Come on, we're nearly there."

Finally, they reached the last door. They hesitated briefly before opening it.

Kimi stepped inside first. "Wow!"

Lark's bedroom was dominated by an enormous

chandelier. It hung gracefully from the ceiling above a tall vase that stood on the floor, filled with crystal flowers. The chandelier was reflected in a full-length mirror that covered an entire wall. The room reminded Kimi of a ballroom, fit for princesses and ballerinas.

Kimi went straight to Lark's bed. "Help me lift the mattress – it's heavy!"

Leena lifted it with both hands while Kimi tucked *The Feathers of Wisdom* into a gap between the mattress and the bed frame.

"Perfect!" Leena slowly lowered the mattress. "She'll never look under there."

"Let's go," said Kimi. "I still worry Lark will appear out of nowhere."

"Before I take you back to Bambaloor, there's someone who'd like to meet you," smiled Leena.

Kimi tucked a strand of hair behind her ear. "Who?"

"The Featherqueen."

Kimi's face lit up. "I'd love that! Yes please!"

Leena reached for her Skyfeathers and threw them up in the air. The feathers settled around them silently. Kimi was so excited to meet the Feather-queen, she could hardly stand still. The room began to spin. She closed her eyes and let out a deep sigh.

But then things went terribly wrong.

Kimi and Leena were in mid-air when they collided with something. They landed in a heap on a pebbly, windswept beach.

"Ouch!" cried Kimi, holding her head. "What was that?"

"Not *what* but *who*," said Leena, clutching her elbow and pointing behind Kimi.

Kimi spun around and covered her mouth.

It was Lark!

Chapter 7

"THAT HURT!" LARK winced, pressing her hand against her forehead. When she noticed Kimi and Leena, she punched the air with delight. "I got you!"

"How did you get here?" cried Leena as she struggled to her feet. "You don't have Skyfeathers any more!"

"I took them from the Featherprince," Lark said icily. "And then I waited for you to use your Sky-feathers again. I knew it was only a matter of time before we bumped into each other."

Kimi turned to Leena. "Can she really do that?"

"Unfortunately, yes," Leena replied.

Lark looked at Kimi. "Who are you, exactly?"

"I'm Kimi. I'm—"

"Actually, I don't want to know."

Taken aback by Lark's rudeness, Kimi took a few brave steps forward but Leena put a hand out to stop her.

"Kimi, don't! You don't know what she's capable of."

"Where's the book, Kimi?" Lark asked menacingly.

"Go away!" Kimi cried. "You'll never find *The Feathers of Wisdom* or the Featherlings' hiding place!"

"Oh, I will," Lark sneered. "And you two are going to help me."

"Never!" Kimi and Leena said in unison.

Lark's mouth fell open. "I'll teach you to disobey me!" she bellowed. She yanked a black feather from her hair and drew a large circle in the air with it.

The sky turned black and the wind, already sharp and wild, intensified. Lightning flashed above their heads.

Lark cackled and drew several smaller circles in the air. The ground began to rumble and shake.

"We've got to get away from her!" Leena shouted in Kimi's ear. "Now!"

The friends dropped to their knees and began to crawl. The furious wind whipped up the sand, making it difficult to see. They kept crawling, further and further away from the beach, until they came to a secluded copse. Kimi noticed a tree hollow that was big enough for the two of them. They crawled inside and sighed with relief.

"I've never seen a Featherling so angry," said Leena.

"I've never seen *anyone* so angry," Kimi agreed. "Can't we use Skyfeathers to disappear from here?"

"Not when it's like this out there. It's not safe to use them when the sky's angry."

They sat in silence, listening to the roaring storm Lark had conjured.

"So this is what it must feel like," said Kimi a little while later.

Leena looked puzzled. "What do you mean?"

"Your life. Hiding from Lark. Every single day."

"We're tired of living like this," Leena said softly. "I wish there was something we could do …"

Kimi began to fidget in the tight space. "I've got an idea! You may not like it, but hear me out."

"Go on."

"Can you call the Featherlings? Ask them to come here?"

Leena flinched. "I don't understand."

"Is there a way to summon the Featherlings?" Kimi asked again.

"You want me to call the Featherlings here? To Lark?"

"Yes."

"All of them? Even the Featherqueen?"

"*Especially* the Featherqueen," Kimi replied.

"Why? You know she's very weak."

"Leena, listen. I think it's time the Featherlings stopped hiding, don't you? You need to confront Lark once and for all."

Leena bit her lip as she considered Kimi's suggestion. "But Lark's so much stronger than the Featherqueen. She won't stand a chance against Lark's dark powers."

Kimi put her hands on Leena's shoulders. "Not alone, no. But if all the Featherlings stand up to Lark, that could change everything."

"All right, I'll do it," Leena sighed nervously. "I just hope you're right."

Kimi popped her head outside. "The wind's calming down. You've got to summon the Featherlings before Lark finds us," she urged Leena.

"There," said Leena as she crawled out of the tree hollow. "That hill's perfect. They'll see my sign from there."

"Your sign? What's that?"

"There's no time to explain. Follow me."

A few minutes later, they reached the top of the hill and immediately spotted Lark.

"Lark's seen us! She's coming!" cried Kimi.

"Stand back!" said Leena. She took off her feather-shaped necklace and held it in the palm of her hand. With her other hand she reached into her pocket for Skyfeathers.

"Hurry up, Leena! Lark's getting closer!"

Leena nodded sternly then threw her necklace and the Skyfeathers high in the air. The moment the necklace and the Skyfeathers collided, glowing sparks filled the air and an enormous purple feather appeared above their heads.

"The sign!" whispered Kimi.

"Every Featherling in the land will see this," said

Leena proudly. "They'll know we need help."

Lark was getting closer.

Kimi tapped her foot impatiently. "How long is this going to take, Leena?"

Leena smiled. "They're already here – look!"

Chapter 8

THE SKY WAS filled with Featherlings. Their dresses and robes fluttered noisily in the wind.

"I didn't know Featherlings could fly!" said Kimi.

"We can, but only with the help of our magical necklaces," Leena replied. "We can't all use Skyfeathers at the same time. You saw what happened with Lark earlier. We'd bump into each other and get hurt."

In the meantime, an ecstatic Lark had reached the top of the hill. "I don't believe it! This is perfect – just perfect!" she shrieked, rubbing her bejewelled hands together. "I'll be the new Featherqueen before the day is over!"

Kimi felt a strange quiver in her stomach. She ran her hands through her hair. *What if all the Featherlings in the Land of Feathers can't defeat Lark? Have I just put them all in danger?*

Clutching their necklaces, the Featherlings landed quickly on the hilltop. When they saw Lark, some gasped, some squeezed their eyes shut, but most just stared at her in disbelief.

Kimi was relieved to see that the Featherprince and the Elders were unharmed after their encounter with Lark in the tower.

The Featherprince had his arms around his

mother, the Featherqueen. He gave Leena a scornful look. "Leena, what are you doing?"

"Don't be scared, we've got a plan!" Leena replied, loud enough for all on the hill to hear.

"Huh!" Lark rolled her eyes and slowly began to make her way towards the Featherqueen. The Featherlings recoiled in fear as Lark brushed past them.

"We've called you here today," Kimi began, hoping she sounded more confident than she felt, "because it's time the Featherlings stopped living in fear. It's time you stood up to Lark!"

Before any of the shocked Featherlings could answer, Lark's malicious laughter filled the air. "I've been searching for you for years," she said. "And now, just like that," – she clicked her fingers – "you're here!" She stood only a few inches away from the frail, helpless Featherqueen. "Say goodbye to your queen," she said with so much venom in her voice, Kimi nearly lost her resolve.

The Featherlings cried out in protest.

"ENOUGH!" Lark screamed and raised her black feather threateningly. "Just look at my sister! Does she look like a powerful Featherqueen to you?"

"Lark, please don't do this," the Featherqueen whispered weakly.

But Lark ignored the Featherqueen. "With me as your new queen, the Featherlings will be unstoppable! We'll become more powerful than you can possibly imagine!"

The Featherqueen was doubled over with pain. She reached out and touched Lark's hand. "It's not our fault that you were banished from the home we once shared … Let us live in peace," she begged. "Lark, please stop hunting us."

Lark shrugged off the Featherqueen's touch. "I'll lead you to treasures," she continued. "We'll fight and defeat our enemies, we'll—"

"The only enemy we have is *you!*" cried a small Featherling, peeking out from behind her mother's robe.

"How dare you speak to me like that?" shrieked Lark. Her face was flushed with anger.

A small crowd of Featherlings rushed forward to protect the little Featherling and her mother. But it was too late.

Lark closed her eyes and lifted her arms towards the sky. She began to mutter something under her breath.

Anguished cries filled the air. Kimi watched in dismay as Featherlings turned to flee.

Lark's chanting grew louder and louder. "*Feather-root! Feather-root!*"

And then, one by one, the Featherlings froze on the spot. They couldn't move!

Lark's ear-splitting laughter erupted again. It chilled Kimi to the core.

She frantically ran between the stuck Featherlings, tugging and pulling at them, but it was in vain. They remained rooted to the spot.

"There must be something you can do!" she said to Leena, panic in her voice.

"We're not strong enough … this was a mistake. Lark's won!"

Out of the corner of her eye, Kimi saw that Lark had turned her attention back to the Featherqueen.

"You never believed in me, sister," Lark said, her jaw tight. "And now look at you." A satisfied grin spread across her face. "You're weak, broken, pathetic and powerless."

Kimi darted towards the sisters. She leaned close to the Featherqueen's ear. "Think!" she whispered. "You're the Featherqueen. You *must* know something Lark doesn't …"

The Featherqueen raised her weary eyes and Kimi saw that she was too weak to fight.

Think, Kimi, think! "Is there no spell you can think of to set you free?" she asked. "A spell from *The Feathers of Wisdom*, perhaps?"

The Featherqueen remained silent. She slowly shook her head. Next to her, the Featherprince buried his head in his hands.

Lark raised her black feather once more and pointed it at the Featherqueen.

Quick as a flash, Kimi stepped in front of the Featherqueen, shielding her.

"Move!" barked Lark.

"I won't!" Kimi answered defiantly. "You're *not* the Featherqueen! You've been banished, you've no right to—"

"That's it, Kimi!" cried the Featherqueen, much to everyone's surprise. "There *is* a spell, you're right … a spell Lark can't possibly know or reverse ... a spell created by our father on the day he banished her."

"The *Five-Kingdom* spell!" said the Featherprince. "You're right, Mother!"

Lark grimaced and narrowed her eyes to slits. "You're lying," she hissed but, for once, she didn't sound sure of herself.

The Featherqueen gathered her strength. She stood up straight and fixed her eyes on Lark.

> *"Spirits of our land,*
> *Hear me when I say,*
> *With Feathers of the Sky*
> *Carry her away.*
>
> *Five kingdoms around us*
> *Will keep us safe and sound.*
> *Featherlings will live in peace,*
> *Evil shall not be crowned."*

Lark's eyes widened in surprise.

The Featherqueen raised her arms high above her head. She began to clap, and signalled the Featherlings to do the same. The clapping gradually became louder and faster.

Lark looked horrified, and staggered backwards. She tripped and fell hard on the ground.

The Featherqueen didn't take her eyes off Lark. She repeated the spell.

> *"Spirits of our land,*
> *Hear me when I say,*
> *With Feathers of the Sky*
> *Carry her away.*
>
> *Five kingdoms around us*
> *Will keep us safe and sound.*
> *Featherlings will live in peace,*
> *Evil shall not be crowned."*

Lark cried out and covered her ears. "No! Please stop!" she begged, struggling to stand up.

The clapping was now louder than ever. Kimi

joined in too.

Lark stumbled around unsteadily, searching for her black feather on the ground. Clumsily, she picked it up and pointed it at the Featherqueen again. She opened her mouth to speak.

Abruptly, the clapping stopped. The sudden silence was deafening.

Only a tiny whimper came from Lark's mouth.

The Featherlings reached for their Skyfeathers. Kimi was surprised to see that instead of throwing them in the air, they blew them towards Lark. Thousands of Skyfeathers roared and swirled around Lark, who waved her arms frantically.

"No! Stop! Please!" she wailed.

But the Featherlings had started to clap again. The thunderous noise continued until the feathers completely engulfed Lark. And then ... she was gone!

Lark's disappearance broke the *Feather-root* spell. The Featherlings joyfully embraced each other, then all eyes turned to their queen.

"We'll never have to worry about Lark again." The Featherqueen gave a broad smile. "Our five neighbouring kingdoms will never let her cross their borders to reach us. Lark will never return. We're free!"

Chapter 9

AFTER THEIR VICTORY over Lark, the Featherlings returned to their cave behind the waterfalls.

"I know this might sound strange, but I'll miss this place." The Featherqueen sighed as she showed Kimi around. "But as you can see, it's rather small. And now, with Lark gone, it's time we moved on ..."

The Featherlings were packing up their belongings, ready to start a new life somewhere else. A new life without Lark. A new life without fear.

"Where will you go?" Kimi

asked, stepping aside to let a Featherling carrying a heavy basket on her head pass.

"Back to the south," the Featherqueen replied with rosy cheeks, glowing with happiness. "We'll rebuild our old lives. We can't wait to get started!"

"That sounds wonderful. I'm happy for you."

"Thank you, Kimi. We couldn't have done it without you. We'll always be grateful to you for saving us," the Featherqueen said, beckoning Leena over.

Leena handed Kimi a soft, feather-shaped bag. "A little present from the Featherlings."

Kimi untied the string and looked inside. "Skyfeathers!"

"Take these feathers back to your world and keep them safe. One day you might need *our* help," said the Featherqueen, a mysterious smile on her face.

"Thank you!" said Kimi. "I'll treasure them. And I hope we'll meet again someday."

"We will," said the Featherqueen. "I'm sure of it."

Leena and Kimi travelled back to the old mill in Bambaloor.

It had turned into a beautiful summer's day, with clear blue skies and warm sunshine. The moment Leena opened the door of the mill, sunlight filled the dark room and she burst out singing.

Not wanting to interrupt her friend, Kimi perched on an old sack.

"Isn't this wonderful?" said Leena. "I love the sunshine, and I can't help singing when I see such beauty. Living behind the waterfall, we hardly ever saw the sun."

Kimi slapped her forehead. "I should've known it was you singing! Did you know, everyone in the forest can hear you? They've been wondering who on earth it is!"

Leena laughed out loud. "I had no idea! I just can't help it. I'm so sorry!"

"It's OK," said Kimi. "There are worse ways to start the day than listening to you sing."

"Well, thank you! Look, while you're here," Leena

continued sheepishly, "can I show you something?"

"Of course."

Leena pulled a sheet off a rusty trunk. She opened the lid and stepped aside to let Kimi have a look. Inside the trunk were bottles of sunscreens, thermos flasks, head torches, sleeping bags and a whole lot more!

"I took these from some of the tents," Leena said. "But I'll return them all," she added quickly. "I promise."

Kimi didn't understand. "Why did you take them?"

"I just wanted to know what they were. There are so many wonderful things in your world that I've never seen before."

All the missing things! That's the final mystery of Bambaloor solved! Kimi thought happily as she knelt down next to Leena to rummage through her stash of camping gear.

"Let's start with this one. What's this?" asked Leena, holding up a long, thin tube.

Kimi laughed. "It's a pump."

Leena stared blankly at Kimi.

"You know ... to blow up a bike's tyres?" said Kimi.

"A *what* to do *what*?" she asked, then she and Kimi collapsed into a heap of giggles.

Kimi and Leena returned the items to their rightful owners and spent all the time they could together.

Leena wanted to know everything about Kimi's world and Kimi enjoyed teaching her friend about magazines, video games, ice rinks and cinemas.

As for Kimi, she loved hearing more about the Featherlings, their special powers, spells and customs. She couldn't get enough of Leena's marvellous tales about the Land of Feathers. She already missed the Featherqueen and the kind Featherlings.

And then one foggy morning it was time to say goodbye. Kimi ran through the forest to the old mill, where they had arranged to meet. They hugged each other and promised to meet again next summer.

"I can't wait to come back next year," Felix said as they set off on the long journey back home.

"Me neither," said Kimi, looking back one last time. Invisible to everyone else, Leena was standing outside the mill, waving to her.

"See you soon," Kimi mouthed to her friend then watched her throw Skyfeathers in the air. The next moment, Leena was gone.

Kimi's dad turned around. "Did you have a good time, Kimi?"

"I did." She smiled. "It was the best holiday ever!"